LITTLE MAN
LITTLE MAN

LITTLE MAN LITTLE MAN

a story of childhood

James Baldwin

with illustrations by Yoran Cazac

Edited by **NICHOLAS BOGGS** and **JENNIFER DEVERE BRODY**

Foreword by Tejan Karefa-Smart * *Afterword by* Aisha Karefa-Smart

Duke University Press * *Durham and London* * 2018

Library of Congress Cataloging-in-Publication Data
Names: Baldwin, James, 1924–1987, author. |
Cazac, Yoran, illustrator. | Boggs, Nicholas, [date] editor. |
Brody, Jennifer DeVere, editor.
Title: Little man, little man : a story of childhood / by James
Baldwin and Yoran Cazac ; edited by Nicholas Boggs and
Jennifer DeVere Brody.
Description: Durham : Duke University Press, 2018. |
Includes bibliographical references and index.
Identifiers: LCCN 2018001470 (print) |
LCCN 2018008826 (ebook) |
ISBN 9781478002345 (ebook)
ISBN 9781478000044 (hardcover : alk. paper)
Classification: LCC PS3552.A45 (ebook) |
LCC PS3552.A45 L5 2018 (print) | DDC 813/.54—dc23
LC record available at https://lccn.loc.gov/2018001470

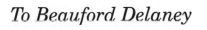

To Beauford Delaney

Contents

The editors would like to thank the following for their support
of this new edition: Gloria Karefa-Smart and Eileen Ahearn of
the James Baldwin Estate; Tejan Karefa-Smart and Aisha Karefa-
Smart; Beatrice Cazac and the Cazac family; Judith Thurman;
Jacqueline Woodson; LeVar Burton; Jade Brooks; Novella Ford and
the Schomburg Center for Research in Black Culture; the National
Museum of African American History and Culture; Sugar Hill
Children's Museum of Art and Storytelling and Broadway Housing
Communities; the Department of English at New York University
and the NYU Center for the Humanities; Dean Richard Sallar and
Associate Dean R. Lanier Anderson of the School of Humanities
and Sciences at Stanford University; and everyone at Duke
University Press, especially Olivia Polk, Amy Ruth Buchanan,
Laura Sell, Jessica Ryan, Jennifer Schaper, and Ken Wissoker.

Little Man, Little Man: We the Children

Tejan Karefa-Smart

The day the box of books arrived marked a wonderful turning point in our childhood adventures on 137 West 71st Street.

Number 137 was our four-story, converted brownstone fortress that sat "smack in the middle of the Block." We could not have known that besides being our own childhood wonderland-village, it would become a travelers' haven and a sojourners' gateway for the who's who of the now-renowned "voices of power" movements in the early and mid-1970s. Our brownstone fortress helped to feed their momentum, acting as meeting place and makeshift home, and we, the children of the household, were definitely not going to miss out on any of this great stuff. We stood steadfast at the gateway to check out every wandering trailblazer that entered our domain: the ever-watchful artist-guardians, musicians, painters, sculptors, and real-life poets who came through every so many moons and left us a bounty of their latest gleanings.

Our building—inside its rooms and walls—was a flourishing pagoda and a wayfarers' harbor for soul-moving works of art. By the time *Little Man, Little Man* dropped into our world, our mother, Gloria, had already weaned us off of a series of Dr. Seuss's Cats-in-hats, Red Fish and Blue Fish, Hortons-hearing-whos, Sam-I-ams, running Jacks and Janes, and whatever bedtime fodder that the New York City Board of Education had PS 199 shoveling us at that time. The kind of textbooks that lacked a vital depth of history and identity for us as Black children and that had no intention of letting on that we might one day be anything more than inner-city kids.

But by the grace of intuitive intervention, we were now being influenced by much more intimate and reflective children's stories. We entered a world of storytelling that placed us on imaginative journeys and took us way above and beyond our school-prescribed reading levels. Besides having this entire arc of artistic voices, we were constantly being fed books of all kinds by our aunts, uncles, and family friends. We shared a single book titled *Contemporary African Literature*, a book full of traditional tales and ancestral proverbs that kept us wildly engaged and intrigued throughout our elementary school years. One particular favorite was the colorfully illustrated "Why Mosquitoes Buzz in People's Ears," a rhythmic nature-tale about the palava-causing consequences of wanton hearsay and gossip. Another was "Mufaro's Beautiful Daughters," a royal tale that illustrated the virtue of a woman's inner beauty over selfish vanity.

Around the same time that our revolving world of words and ideas was being refashioned by this newfound curriculum, we began to notice that whenever Uncle Jimmy came to the brownstone to visit the family, his usually unannounced arrivals would attract a dynamic chorus of voices into our grandmother's apartment. Some of these visitors were our familiar and recognized kinfolk, that is, our uncles, aunts, and cousins of all ages and rank. These were the close and trusted— family friends and relatives who, by now, had become savvy at assuming their reserved places at the threshold of whatever loud conversation was keeping the housing rocking late into the night.

My sister Aisha and I, along with our cousins of similar age, would hover and scan from our just-above-waistline vantage, marveling at how heartily these strangers invaded the 137 village-fortress, apartment 1B, breaching the sacred couch space in the main living room and our Grandma Berdis's sanctum sanctorum—her kitchen.

To our delight, there was no such thing as grown folks' business when Uncle Jimmy was at home and we, the children, mingled and reveled freely among the whiskey and wine sippers. Amid the hum and rush of the many voices, we were amused by the sudden dominant octaves of the womenfolk, the spontaneous pulling of rank by the heavyweights, the taunting *woahs*, *ooOOHHs*, and *ahhhHS*, and the sharp verbal quips that triggered sudden bursts of laughter.

We were the few child-witnesses to what we now know to be some of the most fabulously arranged social jam sessions that ever existed. We were soon sufficiently informed to know—and to opine in our classrooms—that our Uncle Jimmy was *James Baldwin*! And that he possessed a magical power over letters and words, hence the ability to make whole new ideas come into the world with his books. Yes— *our* Uncle Jimmy was a *famous* writer. A celebrated literary artist or (as we would boast to our friends, schoolmates, and teachers)—"An Author."

One fabulous day, surrounded by all that hum and buzz from a jam session in full swing, Uncle Jimmy exited the Japanese screened doors of Grandma's bedroom. I took hold of one of his free arms and yelled:

"Uncle Jimmy! . . . Uncle JIMMY! . . .

When you gonna write a book about MeeeeEEE!?"

This book, *Little Man, Little Man*, was his answer.

It has managed to travel with me through those childhood years and into my adult life as a book of code. The very real people, places, circumstances, and life events that TJ encounters in this story of childhood, the everyday "Music up and down the street," has become for me the rhythm of my own movement through a colorful, wild world.

Introduction

Nicholas Boggs and Jennifer DeVere Brody

In 1976 James Baldwin published *Little Man, Little Man*. His collaborator on the book was a French artist named Yoran Cazac. This experimental, illustrated literary work, subtitled "A Story of Childhood," was ostensibly written as a children's book. The book's jacket cover, however, billed it as a "child's story for adults," and it was precisely this genre-bending aesthetic that confounded readers at the time. When Julius Lester reviewed it for the Children's Book Section of the *New York Times,* he lamented that while there were "brilliant flashes of the Baldwin many of us love," the book has "no storyline," "lacks intensity and focus," and thus fails as a work of children's literature.[1] But now, forty years later, this new edition allows us to rethink the place of *Little Man, Little Man* in the literary career of one of this country's most important writers. More specifically, when viewed from another perspective it is the book's "lack of focus" that gives us a way to think about its success in confronting what Baldwin famously called "the conundrum of color."[2]

The fact that *Little Man, Little Man* went quickly and quietly out of print, and its subsequent relegation to the footnotes of Baldwin's career, has effectively erased its importance to Baldwin, who called it a "celebration of the self-esteem of black children."[3] As this volume's foreword lovingly details, the original impetus for the book was Baldwin's nephew Tejan, who emerges in the story as the four-year-old protagonist, TJ. It is also a book that bears witness to Baldwin's own past and birthright.

As Baldwin told a French journalist in 1974 while he was in the middle of working on *Little Man, Little Man* in his adopted home in

Saint Paul-de-Vence in the south of France, "I never had a childhood. I was born dead."[4] Much as he did in many of his brilliant essays, Baldwin was drawing from his own experiences growing up black and poor in Harlem to dramatize his larger point, that one of the effects of structural and institutional racism is that black children, too often deprived of the resources and opportunities organized to privilege white children, are born into a kind of social death. To counteract this dominant narrative, *Little Man, Little Man* celebrates and explores the challenges, joys, and imaginative resources Baldwin associates with black childhood in Harlem, both his own experiences and those of his nieces and nephews. In doing so, this "child's story for adults" "dances along with a child's rhythm and resilience, making an unforgettable picture as it looks to those who are black, poor, and less than four feet high."[5]

The canon of twentieth-century African American children's literature stretches from W. E. B. Du Bois's monthly children's magazine, *The Brownie's Book* (1920–21), through Langston Hughes's *The Pasteboard Bandit* (1935) and Julius Lester's *To Be a Slave* (1969), to Faith Ringgold's *Tar Beach* (1980) and Toni Morrison's *The Big Box* (1999). While many of these works, like children's literature in general, were written with both adult and child readers in mind, part of what makes *Little Man, Little Man* so noteworthy for its time is its self-aware presentation as a "child's story for adults" that tackles such mature themes as poverty, police brutality, crime, intergenerational relations, addiction, racism, and social marginality through the voice and vision of a black child.

Beginning with its playful opening scene, *Little Man, Little Man* is narrated in the black vernacular style of the Harlem neighborhood where Baldwin grew up as it follows a day in the life of three children—TJ and his seven-year-old friend, WT, and an eight-year-old black girl named Blinky:

> Music all up and down this street, TJ runs it every day. TJ bounce his ball against the sidewalk, hard as he can, sending it as high in the sky as he can, and rising to catch it. Sometimes he misses and has to roll into the street. A couple of times a car almost run him over. That ain't nothing. He going

to be a bigger star than Hank Aaron one of these days. Soon as he get a little bit older, he going to jump the roofs. (2–3)

In his essay "If Black English Isn't a Language, Then Tell Me What Is?," it is precisely the fate of black children that Baldwin turns to in order to make his claim for the necessity of celebrating the beauty of the language of his childhood and youth:

> It is not the black child's language that is despised. It is his experience. A child cannot be taught by anyone who despises him, and a child cannot afford to be fooled. A child cannot be taught by anyone whose demand, essentially, is that the child repudiate his experience, and all that gives him sustenance, and enter a limbo in which he will no longer be black, and in which he knows he can never become white. Black people have lost too many children that way.[6]

If language in general, as Baldwin claims in this essay, "is a political instrument, means and proof of power . . . and the most vivid and crucial key to identity," then the black vernacular voice in *Little Man, Little Man* engages in a strategic resistance to both standard English and the cultural messages of that language system to imagine a different story of black childhood, one that is truly unlike anything that came before or after it. That it does so begs the question of how such an unusual book came into being in the first place.

*　*　*

In the late 1960s and early 1970s Baldwin made multiple trips from his home in the south of France to see his family in New York. During one of these visits, his nephew Tejan implored his famous uncle to write a book about him. Around the same time, in 1971, Baldwin renewed his friendship with Yoran Cazac, a white French artist he had met in Paris back in 1959 through their mutual friend, the black American painter Beauford Delaney. Delaney had mentored a young Baldwin in New York City and later served as a champion for Cazac during his early career in Paris. But now Delaney was suffering from the early stages of schizophrenia in a hospital outside of Paris. Both Baldwin and Cazac were devastated.[7]

As Baldwin finally sat down to write a book about his nephew, he decided that Cazac should provide the illustrations. He also decided that they should dedicate it to the ailing Delaney, and the vision of black childhood showcased in the book's pages clearly bears the imprint of Delaney's influence on writer and artist alike. Baldwin tells a famous anecdote of when he was a teenager standing on Broadway and Delaney told him to look down at the gutter. When Baldwin told him that he saw nothing, Delaney told him to "look again." Then Baldwin saw something spectacular: the reflection of the buildings in the "oil moving like mercury in the black water of the gutter," distorted and radiant. "The reality of his seeing caused me to begin to see," Baldwin explained.[8] Cazac had never been to the United States, let alone Harlem, but Baldwin felt this lack of knowledge would actually help Cazac to "see" Harlem with the fresh eyes Delaney had taught him to value. Still, he knew he would have to educate Cazac about African American life and his family in Harlem in order to provide a blueprint from which he could craft his imaginative vision for the book.

Baldwin showed Cazac a number of sources, including a copy of *The Black Book* (1974), the groundbreaking compilation of words and images drawn from African American history. He also shared photographs of his family as models for characters in the book, including his nephew Tejan and his niece Aisha Karefa-Smart, who wrote the afterword for this edition. These sources, along with Baldwin's conversational descriptions of the neighborhood, allowed Cazac to begin work on capturing a Harlem that he had never seen or experienced. After finishing a full draft of the images in crayon, Cazac realized he needed to work with pencil and watercolor instead, as they would allow him, as he put it, to better "imagine the unimaginable." The final, published version was a series of illustrations characterized by sketchy lines and bleeding colors, from the faces of neighbors sitting on their stoops to the streetscapes of Lenox Avenue itself. It was Harlem and it was not Harlem. Or, rather, it was a Harlem distorted and made strangely, unexpectedly beautiful, mirroring Baldwin's experience when he heeded Delaney's imperative to "look again" and discovered hidden beauty in the dirty puddle of water so many years earlier. In doing so, Baldwin and Cazac enacted Delaney's abiding lesson in the art of seeing differently by asking readers to revalue and find beauty in what has been routinely cast aside as marginal, irrelevant, and even ugly by dominant culture—namely the lives and landscapes of urban black children.

* * *

Throughout *Little Man, Little Man* the character Blinky, and her "blinking" eyeglasses in particular, carries the imprint of Delaney's lesson on Baldwin and Cazac's collaborative vision for the book. As such, we might also think of her as the principal vehicle for the book's primer on how to read "the conundrum of color." As the children move through Harlem together, playing ball, skipping rope, and running errands for neighbors, Blinky increasingly acts as a surrogate sister figure looking out for the welfare of WT and the younger TJ. At first, however, her eyeglasses are a source of skepticism for TJ since he can't see out of them himself, and "some white folks at school" bought them for her (a possible nod to W. E. B. Du Bois, for whom the notion of double consciousness served as a rationale for what he saw as the need for children's literature tailored specifically for black children). But several pages later TJ is already coming to understand that Blinky's own skin "color changing all the time. She always make TJ think of the color of sun-light when your eyes closed and the sun inside your eyes. When your eyes is open, she the color of real black coffee, early in the morning" (11). TJ's dawning realization of the problem of defining the color "black" echoes Baldwin's description of the lesson he learned from Delaney on Broadway: that day he learned that "to stare at a leaf long enough, to try to apprehend the leaf, was to discover many colors in it; and though black had been described to me as the absence of light, it became very clear to me that if this were true, we would never have been able to see the colour; black."[9] Or as Cazac revealed when describing his use of color and light in the book, and why it features characters whose faces sometimes appear only partially painted: "In the full light, no one is fully black or fully white."

Ultimately this story is a story set in an urban world populated by characters whose vision gives us a way of seeing the world as we are not usually taught to see it.[10] This work insists there are messages that we learn early and that intervention must be aimed at a child's understanding even if written for an "adult audience." In this way, we can see how this book is "a child's story *for* adults" (emphasis added). The book's form encourages readers to see *through* the child's perspective: in watercolor, as if they are wearing Blinky's glasses that make everything look like it was rained on. In the process, readers are placed in the position of being "black, poor, and less than four feet high" as the book teaches them to "look again" and experience the social ills represented in the book—violence, economic disparity, alcoholism and drug abuse, and the distortions of mass media—from the perspective of a black child, who, it is important to note in closing, is not innocent.

Throughout his writing Baldwin insisted that all Americans—including children—should rid themselves of a false belief in "innocence," as that prevented them from wrestling with the racism of the nation's past, present, and future. He wrote, "People who shut their eyes to reality simply invite their own destruction, and anyone who insists on remaining in a state of innocence long after that innocence is dead turns himself into a monster."[11] Part of what is so remarkable about *Little Man, Little Man,* as a "child's story for adults," is how seriously Baldwin and Cazac take the intellectual and emotional potential of their readers, both children and adults, to eschew this culturally willed innocence and instead open their eyes to the social ills of their time and, in the process, imagine a different, previously unimaginable future.

For all these reasons and more, it is safe to say that there is no other book out there quite like *Little Man, Little Man*, which is perhaps why it has been misunderstood and overlooked for so long. Yet contrary to the review in *Book World* that described the book as "an exciting, perhaps an important book, but a book with one fatal flaw: its concept of audience is flawed,"[12] it may be that it has been the book's audience, instead, that has had a skewed view of the book's deceptively complex rendering of the language and experience of black childhood in Harlem. With this edition of *Little Man, Little Man*, we invite a new generation of students, teachers, Baldwin scholars, and all readers to "look again" and to make this decision for themselves.

Notes

1. Julius Lester, "Little Man, Little Man," *New York Times Book Review*, September 4, 1977, p. 22.

2. In the preface to *Notes of a Native Son*, Baldwin writes: "The conundrum of color is the inheritance of every American, be he/she legally or actually Black or White. It is a fearful inheritance, for which untold multitudes, long ago, sold their birthright. Multitudes are doing so, until today. . . . Something like this, anyway, has something to do with my beginnings. I was trying to locate myself within a specific inheritance and to use that inheritance, precisely, to claim the birthright from which that inheritance had so brutally and specifically excluded me." See James Baldwin, "Introduction to New Edition," in *Notes of a Native Son* (Boston: Beacon Press, 1984), p. xii.

3. David Leeming, *James Baldwin: A Biography* (New York: Henry Holt, 1994), p. 330.

4. "James Baldwin: Entretiens," an unpublished interview, conducted in French by Christian de Bartillat in 1974; cited in James Campbell, *Talking at the Gates: A Life of James Baldwin* (Berkeley: University of California Press, 1991), p. 3.

5. James Baldwin and Yoran Cazac, *Little Man, Little Man: A Story of Childhood* (London: Michael Joseph, Ltd., 1976), jacket description.

6. James Baldwin, "If Black English Isn't a Language, Then Tell Me What Is?," in *The Price of the Ticket: Collected Nonfiction, 1948–1985* (New York: St. Martin's/Marek, 1985), p. 651.

7. The biographical information in this introduction draws on the pioneering work of Baldwin's biographer, David Leeming, in *James Baldwin: A Biography*, and new information gathered in interviews by Nicholas Boggs with Yoran Cazac, on May 17, 2003, at the Kiron gallery and May 18, 2003, in Cazac's studio, both in Paris, France. An earlier version of this introduction appeared in a different form in Nicholas Boggs, "Baldwin and Cazac's 'Child's Story for Adults,'" in Michele Elam, ed., *The Cambridge Companion to James Baldwin* (Cambridge: Cambridge University Press, 2015), pp. 118–132.

8. James Baldwin, "Introduction to Exhibition of Beauford Delaney Opening December 4, 1964, at the Gallery Lambert," *Beauford Delaney: A Retrospective* (New York: Studio Museum in Harlem, 1978), unnumbered page.

9. James Baldwin, "On the Painter Beauford Delaney," in Toni Morrison,

ed., *James Baldwin: Collected Essays* (New York: Library of America, 1998), p. 720.

10. The authors would like to thank Margo Natalie Crawford for her conversations with us about *Little Man, Little Man* and for her thoughtful work on Blinky's role in the book, in particular. Both have greatly influenced the writing of this introduction. See her "Eye-Glasses Blinking: Between James Baldwin and Yoran Cazac," unpublished article. We would also like to thank the anonymous readers of our book proposal at Duke University Press. Their thoughtful comments helped us formulate aspects of this introduction.

11. James Baldwin, "Stranger in the Village," in *The Price of the Ticket*, p. 89.

12. Ann S. Haskell, "Baldwin: Harlem on His Mind," *Book World*, September 11, 1997, E6.

LITTLE MAN
LITTLE MAN

Music all up and down thi.

TJ bounce his ball against the sidewalk hard as he can, sending it as high in the sky as he can, and rising to catch it. Sometimes he misses and has to roll into the street.

2

treet, TJ runs it every day.

A couple of times a car almost run him over. That ain't nothing. He going to be a bigger star than Hank Aaron one of these days. Soon as he get a little bit older, he going to jump the roofs.

He hears Mr Man's record player from the basement. Mr Man is the janitor, he collect the garbage cans. TJ always stumbling into the garbage cans because they on the first floor, right next to where Miss Beanpole lives.

Here he come now, Mr Man, huffing and puffing with them garbage cans, setting them on the side-walk. He try to act like he don't see TJ. He always try to act like he mean. He ain't mean, but he getting pretty old, TJ Mama say he got to be about thirty-seven.

He about the color of chocolate cake without no icing on it. Except when he grin, but he don't hardly never grin, except at TJ and sometime he act like he don't see him. But TJ know he see him, all the time, even when

he look like he ain't looking, and he even grin at WT and
Blinky, too, when he act like he see them. He a real nice
man. Sometime he take them down the basement where
the furnace is and he tell them stories and he give them
ginger snaps and the furnace keep huffing and puffing
just like Mr Man with the garbage cans and it get real
red hot and Mr Man grin with all them teeth and it real
nice then,

he a real, real real nice man.

    He go downstairs now, though, before TJ can throw
him the ball and make him catch it.

    So he bounce the ball back up in the air again and
jump to catch it. This time he catch it right but he got to
fall down on his knees and he scrape one knee.

    Blinky and WT done stopped skipping rope, and
watching him.

TJ don't look at them. He look at his knee. He don't want his Mama to get worried. It not too bad. It bleeding just a little bit. He spit on it and rub it and stand up. It ain't nothing at all.

But Blinky, she just looking from across the street. **Them eye-glasses blinking just like the sun was hitting you in the eye.** TJ don't know why she all the time got them glasses on. She say she can't see without them. Maybe that true, if she say so. But TJ put them on one time and he couldn't see nothing with them on. He couldn't see across the street. Everything looked like it was rained on. So TJ ain't too sure about Blinky. It was some white folks at school bought her them glasses. If *he* can't see out them, how *she* going to see out them? And she older than he is. She eight years old. She ought know better. But she a girl.

WT is seven and ain't no excuse for him at all, skipping rope and following behind Blinky. WT got the right name, he the color of tea after you put in the milk. Blinky, she a funny color.

Her color changing all the time. She always make TJ think of the color of sun-light when your eyes closed and the sun inside your eyes. When your eyes is open, she the color of real black coffee, early in the morning.

A car comes, *wow!* up one end of the street and down the other, gone now, *hey!* And Blinky yells from across the street.

"TJ! You trying to get yourself killed?"

Ain't no reason to answer her and he bounce the ball hard, as hard as he can, back up into the air. It go way, way up, now look at that and you over there skipping rope, I sure hope you all saw that you jive, and he catches the ball as the ball comes down **but it knocks him on his ass.**

It hurt, it hurt him a lot, but he don't want to act like it hurt and so he get up and don't say nothing to Blinky, he act like he ain't heard nothing and he look up and down the street. Where he was born.

This street long. It real long. It a little like the street in the movies or the TV when the cop cars come from that end of the street and then they come from the other end of the street and the man they come to get he in one of

the houses or he on the fire-escape or he on the roof and he see they come for him and he see the cop cars at that end and he see the cop cars at the other end. And then he don't know what to do. He can't go nowhere. And he sweating. And the cops come out their cars and they got their guns and they start coming down the street. Some of them come from that end and some of them come from the other end. They don't know exactly where the man is, but they know he somewhere in this street. TJ live almost smack in the middle of the block. If they come down from that end, the way he facing now, well then, the man might be in *Walter's Bar and Grill* on this side of the street or he might be in the tailor shop on the other side of the street. If he ain't in neither of them places, and the cops keep coming real slow and careful down this long street with their guns out, then he might be in the record store on this side of the street or he might be in the house on the other side of the street.

He might be on one of the fire-escapes, or he might be on the roof. If he on one of them roofs don't care which side of the street he on, he going to

have to run like a mother and jump a roof to get him to another block. But the cops already thought of this and they got their cars in all the other blocks.

And now everybody on the street get real up-tight and the cops move slow and the people don't say nothing but they

watching. If the man ain't
in the record store, then
he in the house next to the
record store or he in the
candy store on the other
side of the street. If he

ain't there, then he in the
next house, or in the church
on the other side of the
street. If he ain't there,
then he in TJ's house, on
this side of the street

or in the house across from
TJ's house. TJ's house in
the middle of the block, so
he turn now and look the
other way.

The cops coming from the other end of this long street got to watch out for their man from the playground on TJ's side of the street or from the empty lot on the other side of the street. He might be in the ice-cream parlor on TJ's side of the street. He might be in Blinky's house, on the other side of the street. He might be in the liquor store, on TJ's side of the street. He might be in the house across from the liquor store. He might be in WT's house, on this side of the street. He might be in the house across from WT.

After that, there the church again.

One thing for sure, by the time the cops get this far they know they got their man. He sweating and running and ducking but he done for. He not going to get off this street alive. Sometime he running down the middle of the street and the guns go *pow!* and *blam!* he fall and maybe he turn over twice before he hiccup and don't move no more. Sometime he come somersaulting down from the fire-escape. Sometime it from the roof, and then he scream.

WT and Blinky done come running across the street, and WT say, "You hurt yourself, man?"

WT always want to sound like he so grown-up.

"No. I ain't hurt myself. Thought you was skipping rope."

Blinky, she just looking with them glasses just a-blinking.

TJ don't bounce the ball this time, though, he a little afraid to have to try to catch it again, now that Blinky and WT on this side of the street. And his behind do hurt him, it hurt him more and more but he act like it ain't nothing.

"Man, we saw you fall down two times, that's why we come on over here. I'm supposed to watch out for you. You know that."

"You ain't got to watch for me," TJ say, and he bounce his ball on the sidewalk but not hard this time, just enough to catch it in his hand.

But he happy, really, that WT standing there, **looking at him with that grown-up frown.** TJ ain't got no brothers and WT like a brother for him. He do look out for TJ, that's true. And TJ bounce the ball a little bit again.

TJ ask WT, "You see me catch it before?"

"I saw you fall on your ass," WT say.

That WT all over. Ask him a simple question and he got to be smart. Sometime TJ wish he had another friend, somebody who wouldn't all the time be being smart with him. But he the smallest boy in the block. Ain't but WT be bothered with him. TJ doubt even Blinky be bothered with him if she wasn't all the time running after WT. WT younger than the other boys, true, but soon he be getting big — he pretty big already, for his age. Then maybe he won't bother with TJ no more, neither.

The other boys, when they in the block, sometimes they play stickball in the street. But mostly they sit on the stoop and they play cards and shoot crap and sometime they get to fighting. They go up to the roof or they go behind the stairs and they shoot that dope in their veins and they come out and sit on the stoop and look like they gone to sleep.

They don't look like they never bother nobody but WT say that that why he look out for TJ, so TJ won't never get to be like that. TJ don't see how he ever going to be like that, but then WT say, just like a real old man, **"They didn't think so, neither."**

WT got a brother older than him and he sit on the stoop like that a whole lot of times.

One time TJ watch WT while he beat on his brother,
he slap him all over his face with both hands hard as he
can, and he curse his brother, he call him every name he
can think of, and his brother just make sounds and spit
coming out his mouth and running down his chin and his
eyes roll up and he move just like them plants TJ saw
under the water, just back and forth and back and forth

like that, just like them plants TJ saw way at the bottom of the water that time when they went to Jones Beach and his Daddy carried TJ out in the water on his back.

Then WT start to crying and he run down the block hard as he can but TJ run after him and catch him in the playground. TJ just sit there on a swing while WT cry and cry and TJ want to say something but he don't know what to say. To tell the truth, he scared. But WT stop crying after a while and he put his hand on TJ's neck and they start to walking. But they don't say a word.

Soon, here come TJ's father up the block, looking for TJ, and he look like he mad but he ain't. He take one look at WT and he take out a handkerchief and he wipe his face. He say, "Your Mama ain't home yet. Come on home and have some cocoa with TJ."

That how come WT got to be TJ's brother. WT father gone. His Mama work till past dark. And lots of times WT stay at the house with TJ.

They hear Mr Man's record player from the basement, and Blinky start go fooling around, and dancing. WT, he do everything Blinky do, and so he start to dancing, too.

"Come on, TJ!" WT say, and TJ start doing his African strut.

WT love to see TJ strut. It crack him up every time.

"Go on, TJ!" WT say, laughing, and just moving to the music, him and Blinky.

TJ move like he in a jungle where **he can't get no satisfaction.**

One thing TJ understand about Blinky. She don't like nothing that wears dresses. She don't hardly never wear a dress herself. She always in blue jeans. Look like she do everything she can to be a boy. But she ain't no boy.

Blinky is a girl. But she don't like girls.

So, when she sees Miss Lee coming up the street, she say, "Here come Miss Lee. Look like she can't hardly walk."

WT and TJ, they both dig Miss Lee. Sometime she send WT to the store alone, but she never send TJ to the store alone. If she see them together, she call them over to her. She stand leaning on the railing and she say, "Which one of you fine men want to go to the store for me?"

TJ always yell first, "Me! I want to go!" — even though he know she ain't going to send him by himself.

Him and WT run over to Miss Lee. She standing behind the railing, at the gate top of the basement steps.

Miss Lee look at him real hard and she say, "Well, all right. But you so little wouldn't nobody never be able to find you if you got lost."

And she look like she really mean it. She real serious. She don't smile a bit, except you can tell she really smiling to herself inside. She having fun. It all in her eyes.

Then she look at WT, and she say, "WT, this little man want to go to the store for me but I'm scared to send him off by himself. He need a big man to go with him. You want to take this little man to the store for me?"

And WT smile, and he say, "Yes ma'am."

Then Miss Lee smile and she say, "Thank you, WT. You are a gallant gentleman." And WT he just puff up like he going to explode.

Then Miss Lee give TJ the money and she tell him what she want. And she make TJ repeat it. Then she say, to WT, "Now, you just make sure that don't nothing happen to him, you hear? Don't want nobody carrying off my little man."

WT say, "I ain't going to let nothing happen to him, Miss Lee."

And then they go off to the store. TJ got the money, so he run. But he just teasing WT. WT can run him faster anyway. But TJ just like to tease WT because Miss Lee give the money to TJ. She didn't give it to WT.

But when they come back from the store, she give WT a nickel. She say, "Now you got to share this with TJ. He the one went to the store."

And then she smile and go on down the stairs. She got a beautiful smile. She real beautiful sometimes. She younger than Mr Man. She got a color like honey and water-melon. She got real long curly black hair. She real skinny. She got real long legs. She married to Mr Man. She live down there with him. They ain't got no children.

Sometimes she sad, true, and that's when Blinky say
she can't hardly walk. That not true. Blinky just don't
like the woman because she never send Blinky to the
store. But sometimes Miss Lee look sad and she walk
like she don't know where she going. But she walk
straight. She don't stagger and stumble. Her eyes is red
sometime and she smell strong, like smoke, and sweet,
like she been eating peppermint candy, and sometime
she smell like licorice. But she always walk straight.

Here she come now up the street, just like Blinky say. She coming from *Walter's Bar and Grill*. She carrying a paper bag. She just like Mr Man. Sometime she see you and sometime she don't.

She open her gate and she walk on down the steps like she don't see them.

Mr Man record player still going, though, and they keep on dancing. WT got a hole in one sneaker. His flesh right on the sidewalk really but he just keep dancing and moving to the music. WT beautiful really.

He a pain but he really beautiful. He know Blinky want to dance and that really why he dancing. But his mind somewhere else. His mind always somewhere else. Like when he skip rope with Blinky, he do it for Blinky but he do it for another reason too. WT going to be a boxer and so he got to train like a boxer. Somebody tell him once that Sonny Liston used to skip rope while he had Night Train on his record player. So now, WT take the rope from Blinky and he start to skipping rope in time to the music.

Miss Beanpole make a sign for TJ to come on over to her window. At first, he act like he don't see her. Blinky and WT busy with each other. So TJ strut over to Miss Beanpole's window.

"Come on in here," she say. "I want you to go to the store for me."

So he run up the stoop, and into the hall. He bump into Miss Lee. She coming up from the basement real fast. She got two bottles in one hand and she throw them in the garbage can outside Miss Beanpole's door.

Then she see him.
"Why, hello there, TJ," she say.
But she act like she don't see him really.

She got a paper bag in her other hand,

but she don't throw that in the garbage can. She keep on
up the stairs, into the building.

TJ a little surprised because the only time he ever see
her upstairs in the building is when she got to sweep
it or mop it down. But she ain't going to sweep or mop
today. She got on a black dress and them high heel shoes
what make her legs look even longer and her hair not
tied up, it hanging loose. When she mop and sweep and
scrub from the top floor to the basement, her hair tied up
and she wear a old sweater and pants and sneakers.

Lot of the time it Mr Man who do it but a lot of the
time he got to be with them garbage cans and he got to
take care of the furnace and he don't like Miss Lee to
clean the roof. Mr Man always clean the roof.

Miss Lee keep on up the stairs. TJ want to ask if he
can help her. He don't know why. She ain't never asked
for no help.

Miss Beanpole live in the house next to TJ's house. She sits in the window most days. But she is tall when she stands up. She is tall when she calls TJ or WT or Blinky to go to the store for her. Then you have to go inside her house. She has a lot of locks on her door. When she opens it, she has to move a long iron stick in the floor. This long iron stick leans against the door when the door is locked. When she opens the door the stick moves back, like the door, and then you are inside.

TJ always afraid Miss Beanpole will pull the stick up out the floor and start beating him over the head with it. She looks like she want to beat somebody.

The inside is dark and Miss Beanpole ain't never dressed. She always in her bath-robe, with her hair tied up. She always tie it up in the same old rag. The rag older than TJ and TJ almost five. TJ know a color when he sees one, he knows green from purple and yellow and green and red from blue, he already learned that, but he don't know what color the rag is. He don't really know what color Miss Beanpole is. She look like she a little bit white and a little bit colored, kind of more white on top than she is around the mouth, but she probably more white than colored. TJ more colored than *she* is. But he don't know about her hair, he never see it. Miss Beanpole is very old. She smells like peanuts.

She never in the street. That why she always send you to the store for what she want. She mostly want a half

pound of this and a quarter pound of that. Then you can't go to the big store, they don't want to hear that — no, you got to go to one of them little stores. One of them is three blocks off and one of them is five blocks off. And then you better not tell nobody because they don't want you going all that far and crossing all them streets and maybe getting yourself run over and going that far out their sight. **But TJ do it all the time.** He just make sure that Blinky don't know. He always wait till she got her back turned, doing something else — she always doing something — and then he just vanish out the block. Time he get back, Blinky know he been gone but ain't no use in her saying nothing, too late. Miss Beanpole buy one pork chop at a time. Then she give you a penny and she close the door. The big iron stick go *blam* against the door and then you hear her locking all the locks. Then she sit down in the window again till it get past dark. TJ don't know what she see out that window but she all the time sitting there.

Today look like she watching Blinky and WT across the street. Blinky skipping rope. WT ain't got no better sense than jump inside the rope with her sometime, *clack-clack, clackety-clack, whish, clack, clackety-clack, whish, clack, clack, clack!* like a fool, thinks TJ, and WT older than him.

Now Miss Beanpole done turned all her locks. TJ hear that iron stick scraping across the floor. Then she open the door but she don't never open it wide.

TJ go on in.

Miss Beanpole lock all them locks and close the door with the stick back in place. She walk to the front room and TJ follow her.

Miss Beanpole got a voice like a man. She say, "How you making it, TJ?"

TJ say, "All right."

He can't call her Miss Beanpole, that ain't her real name. He call her Miss Beanpole she swear he making fun of her. His Daddy told him her real name but he can't never remember it.

Miss Beanpole go to her dresser drawer like always. She take out her purse. It tiny and fat and brown, like a water-bug. She turn her back to TJ, like always, and she snap it open. TJ don't never like to look at her back. When she got her back to him her back go up and her head go down so far he can't hardly see that head-rag and he can hear her fingers moving in that purse like she was blind.

Her fingers go chink and clink and clink-a-chink while her back turned to him. Ain't no light but the light from the window, but Miss Beanpole, she standing in a corner in the dark. Clink-clink. Chink-chink and then it make a kind of rattling sound.

Mr Man done stopped his record player.

TJ look around him. Don't nothing never change in this room, but TJ always look around him when he here. It like a real weird room. Like a room in the movies or the TV where something happened in the room a long time ago and somebody hid in the room and they saw what happened and they still hiding in the room. They see everything in the room like now they can see every bit of change Miss Beanpole is counting out. Ain't nothing so dark but they can't see it. And then they going to jump out and tell what they saw and then something awful happen in the room.

Miss Beanpole got a lot of things in her room. TJ always stand still. He afraid he bump into something. He might even bump into whoever hiding in the room. Maybe that why Miss Beanpole never go out. She afraid of leaving the person alone in the room.

TJ *know* there something hiding in the room. He don't want to bump into nothing. Then he might find out what happened and then Miss Beanpole pull that iron stick up out the floor and beat him over the head with it.

She got shiny flowers on a round table in the middle of the floor. They in a great big green glass with bumps all over it. Look like she dust the flowers every day, way they shine. The table covered with a long brown cloth. Just like the big green glass got bumps all over it, the long brown cloth got tiny holes all in it. It got fringes right down to the floor. Ain't no chairs around this table.

Then, on the wall, in front of where she standing, Miss Beanpole got a big picture of the Lord. He got a kind of pitiful smile on His face but his heart be full of blood and He got one hand raised. There be a blood red hole in the middle of His hand. That where the nail went through His hand when they nailed Him to the cross.

Then, Miss Beanpole got a whole lot of other pictures on the other wall, look like the pictures of people she knew back in the olden days. Most of the people she knew is all smiling. They real dark. They mostly all in white.

On another table, in a corner, she got a big open bible. There a little lamp on this table but it off. And a chair at the table. In front of the window, Miss Beanpole's rocking chair.

TJ going to start school just as soon as the summer over.

Now Miss Beanpole snap her purse shut and put it back in the dresser drawer. She start walking over to TJ with her money in her hand.

TJ don't know why he so scared of her.

But maybe he not really scared. He not scared like he is sometime in the middle of the night when he wake up all of a sudden and he don't hear nobody in the house. Then, he scared. He real scared. He sleep in a room by himself. His Mama and Daddy in the room across the hall. The bathroom next to their room. After that, there the kitchen.

TJ real happy on Sunday mornings, when his Daddy be home all day and TJ and his Mama and Daddy all eat breakfast together in the kitchen. TJ's father is a little like Mr Man, except he much younger. TJ's Mama and Daddy, they laugh a lot on Sunday morning.

TJ's Mama is the most beautiful woman in the whole world. He never see a woman as beautiful as his Mama. Even Blinky say so, and she don't like nothing that wears a dress. She say, "Now, take Miss Lee. She must got a pound of make-up on her face. Mr Man must get real sick every night when he see her take it off. But your Mama, now, she beautiful. And she don't put nothing on her face but water."

And it true. TJ's Mama got a lot of coal-black hair. All she do is comb it with her Afro comb and it stand out on her head and it shine, like a crown. She got a little nose, it all the time wiggling when she laugh. She like to laugh. Her skin the color of peaches and brown sugar. She love TJ and she tell him everything he need to know, like every time he ask her a question she give him a straight answer. She always tell him, if he want to know the answer to something or if something bother him, don't care what it is, don't go creeping around strangers trying to find out, to come to her or his Daddy. She tell him everything about his body, and she tell him about babies. TJ don't really exactly understand everything about that but he know it got to be true if his Mama say so.

And sometime he look at his Mama and Daddy when they laughing in the kitchen Sunday mornings, and he try to understand but he know he don't really. He come out his Mama's belly. Sometime he put his head against her belly. He come from a real warm place.

TJ's Daddy say his Mama spoil him. TJ's Mama say his Daddy spoil him. TJ's Daddy try to act mean, but he ain't mean. Sometime he give TJ a nickel on the sly and

he wink and say, "Don't tell your Mama. This is just between us men." And sometime he take TJ to the movies and he take him to the beach and he took him to the Apollo Theatre, so he could see blind Stevie Wonder.

"I want you to be proud of your people," TJ's Daddy always say.

TJ proud of his people, just like he proud of his Daddy. His Daddy one of them people: they boss people.

When he wake up scared, in the middle of the night, he always got this feeling that maybe something awful done happened to his Mama and Daddy. He listen real hard to hear them breathing. Sometime he listen real hard and he don't hear a sound. Then, he scared. Then, he try to remember what his Daddy told him about that. His Daddy say he don't want no fool for a son, and TJ just being a fool if he think his Mama and Daddy going jump up and leave him. They *can't* leave him. Don't nobody else want him. Then, TJ's Daddy, he laugh, and say, "I reckon *we* the fools."

TJ don't think they going to leave him. He just afraid
something happen to them. He don't know why. It a
feeling come on him all of a sudden, he don't know why.
WT's Daddy gone, don't nobody know where, and WT's
Mama ain't hardly never home. WT got to carry the keys
to the house around his neck. And Blinky live with her
aunt. Her Mama went away with somebody.

So TJ get scared sometime in the middle of the night.
His Daddy say he don't want no cry-baby for a son, so he
don't cry, he just lie in bed, stiff and still.

Then, sometime, he finally hear a noise from their room. He hear one of them get up and go to the bathroom. Then, he go to sleep. But sometime he stay awake till morning if he don't hear no sound.

He don't get up and he don't cry or nothing because TJ's Daddy drive a taxi all day and he need his sleep.

He not scared of Miss Beanpole the way he scared at night. And if he so scared of her, why he all the time in her house? No, he ain't exactly scared. But Miss Beanpole a strange woman. Living down here all by herself and sitting in that window like she waiting for somebody.

Who she waiting for? And she old as time.

She give him the money now and she tell him what she want. She want a quarter pound of cheese and a loaf of bread.

He always say, "That all?"
And she always say,
"Yes. Hurry back."

And sometime she put her hand on his forehead, just for a minute, like she thinking of something else.

Then she march to the door and pull back that stick and unlock the locks.

The minute Blinky see him, she say, "Now, where you fixing to go?"

It funny. When he go to the store for Miss Lee, WT got to go with him and that all right because Miss Lee say so. But when he go to the store for Miss Beanpole, he like to go by himself. He don't want nobody watching out for him. He going to have to go to *school* by himself.

But Blinky see him and WT see him and Miss Beanpole sitting in the window. So he can't just run out the block.

He don't say nothing to Blinky. He say, loud, "WT, I got to go to the store. You want to come with me?"

WT real cool. He look quick at Miss Beanpole, and he say, "Yeah, baby, I come with you." He look quick at Blinky and he give her back the rope and he say, "You want to come, too?" and he look quick at TJ.

Blinky say, "Yeah, I'm coming," and WT say, "Well, let's move it," and they head on out the block. And it all right now.

They got to go one block west, to Seventh Avenue, and then they got to go two blocks down. So they go past *Walter's Bar and Grill* and get to Lenox Avenue. WT hold TJ's hand while they wait for the light.

Then, they cross Lenox Avenue and start

down the long block to Seventh Avenue.

This block always seems real sad and strange to TJ. He ain't never on this block, so he don't know nobody. The women is sitting on the stoops like they ain't got nothing to do, just sitting and looking. The men is standing and walking. Don't look like they got nothing to do neither. Somehow it always seem to be silent on this block. Nobody don't yell at nobody. Nobody play no music. There are three churches on one side of the street. There about four churches on the other side of the street.

TJ hop skip and jump down the block. WT and Blinky right behind him. They pass the liquor store on the corner and they turn left. There the barber shop with the men standing in front of it and the men inside. There the dude outside who sells *Muhammad Speaks*. TJ's father read *Muhammad Speaks* sometime, but then he say, "Don't believe everything you read. You got to *think* about what you read." His Mama say, "But read everything, son, everything you can get your hands on. It all come in handy one day."

TJ don't really understand none of this yet, but she say, "Don't worry. You going to understand it."

The other side of Seventh Avenue all empty. They done torn down all the buildings. Don't nobody know where all the people used to live there moved. It look like winter, far as the eye can see. There a long iron fence all along the avenue. There a sign on the fence that say, This property belong to So-and-So and they going to build something on it when they get ready.

There not many people in the store. It a little store. He a Puerto Rican, the man who run it. TJ ask for the bread and cheese and the man look at him kind of funny but then he smile and he slice the cheese and he give TJ the bread. TJ give him the money and the man smile and say, "*Adios, muchachito!*"

TJ say, "*Adios!*" and WT say, "*Adios!*"

When they get outside TJ want to know what do *adios* mean.

"It mean good-bye," Blinky say — but she ain't said nothing to the man in the store — "He said, *adios, muchachito*. That mean Good-bye, little boy."

"How do you know?" ask TJ.

"I got friends who speak Spanish," Blinky say.

They go back home by another block, and TJ take the bread and cheese in to Miss Beanpole and she give him two cents and she rub his forehead again.

When TJ come out, WT whisper, "How much she give you?"

Miss Beanpole back in her window. WT don't want her to hear him.

"She give me two cents," TJ say, and he look at Blinky real quick. But she act like she don't mind.

"Let's go to the candy store," WT say, and they run down the block, across the street, to the candy store. They buy some bubble gum and they give some to Blinky. Then, they run back across the street and start running down the block.

TJ a little ahead of them.
He running, and then he
bounce his ball hard,
hard as he can, and
it go way up, and
he rise up to
catch it.

He rises up and something comes down, but it is not the ball. It flashes, flashes, flashes over his head like lightning, like thunder it crashes at his feet.

It like a big explosion, like a bomb falling on him,

and TJ scream and start to cry, he on his ass, on the sidewalk, crying. WT just come running. And Blinky scream. WT lift TJ up, and he say, "You hurt, man? You hurt?" There glass all over the sidewalk. There some glass even in TJ's hair and WT brush it out real careful and it make a funny kind of sound when it hit the sidewalk. "You lucky it didn't hit you in the eye," WT say, just like a real old man. TJ ain't bleeding. He ain't hurt none, but he still crying and he done lost his ball.

But Blinky say,

"WT, your foot! Look at your foot!

You standing in a pool of blood!"

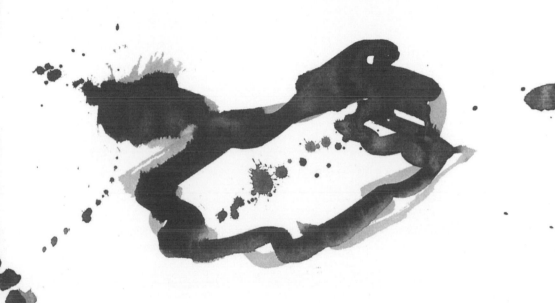

And they all look down at the ground, and it true. WT got that hole in his sneaker and he done stepped on the glass and his foot be bleeding something awful.

TJ stop crying because he scared for WT, WT didn't say nothing but he look like he going to vomit.

"Come on," Blinky say, "Come on."

She take WT by one hand and TJ hold him by
the other and she lead them down the steps, to the
basement, to Mr Man's house.

Blinky yell, "Mr Man! Hey, Mr Man! Come on out
here!"

It dark in the basement, nobody around. WT start to
shiver.

"Mr Man!" Blinky yell. "Mr Man!"

Mr Man come out the furnace room, real slow, and he
switch on the light and he look at them.

At first he say, "What's the matter?" like he don't want
to be bothered, and then he say, "Come on in here!" and
he open the door on the other side of the basement hall,
where he live with Miss Lee. He take them from the
kitchen to the bedroom and he stretch WT out on the bed.

80

He take off WT's sneaker and he say, "What happened?"

WT don't say nothing. His skin the color of a lemon. But he don't cry. He hold TJ tight by one hand.

"A bottle fell off the roof," Blinky say.

Mr Man look up. He look scared, all of a sudden, and sick.

"Off *this* roof?" he ask Blinky.

"I think so," Blinky say. "We was just about in the front of the house."

WT's foot just keep dripping and dripping blood. It a big cut.

"You got bandages?" Blinky say. Her glasses just shining, like they scared as she is.

"Go see if you can find my wife," Mr Man say.

Blinky run out, and Mr Man get up and go to the kitchen and come back with a basin of cold water and a big towel.

"Don't be scared," he say to WT. "It ain't nothing. It just bleeding a lot. We stop that in a minute."

He pull WT to the side of the bed, so he can get his foot in the water. TJ just standing there.

Mr Man look up, and he say, "Hold him up, TJ."

So TJ put his arm around WT and hold him, and Mr Man start to washing WT's foot. The water turn dark with blood. WT catch his breath and start to shivering again.

"It ain't nothing," Mr Man say, again. "Just be cool. We have it fixed in a minute."

He start to drying WT's foot with the towel. When he dry it, the blood still coming but not so much as before. Mr Man look at WT's foot real careful and he run his fingers along the cut and WT scream.

"Now, be cool," say Mr Man. "I just got to make sure ain't no glass in this cut." And he wash WT's foot again.

Then, Blinky and Miss Lee come in. Miss Lee look scared to death. She look like she don't know what she doing. She don't say nothing. She go straight to the bathroom. She come back with some bandages and peroxide and iodine.

She come to the bed, and she say, "Let me do it."

Mr Man move away and stand up and he look down on Miss Lee in a very strange way. It like he want to hit her, and, at the same time, he want to kiss her. It like he want to strangle her. It like he almost going to cry.

Miss Lee say, "This going to sting a little, WT. But I know you going to take it like a man."

She put some peroxide on some cotton and she rub WT's foot. WT start to shivering again, and he lean hard against TJ. The peroxide make bubbles on WT's foot. Miss Lee do this about two or three times and the bleeding almost stop. Then she say, "Now, hold on, WT!" and she paint the cut with iodine. WT's face covered with sweat and he lean harder than ever on TJ, but he don't say nothing.

Then, Miss Lee start to bandaging the foot, real careful.

Blinky ask, "Did you used to be a nurse?"

Miss Lee don't look up. She keep on with what she doing. Then, she say, "Yes." She look quick at Mr Man. "Before I got married."

Mr Man sigh, and he look more evil than ever, but he hold his peace.

Miss Lee cut up some adhesive tape and she wrap it around the bandage to keep it in place.

84

"There," she say, and she look up at WT. "You a real brave little man." She stand up and she move TJ out the way and she make WT lay back down on the bed. She smile, and say, "We ain't got no gin. But we can give you a Pepsi Cola. Would you like that?"

WT say, "Yes," and he try to smile.

Mr Man say, "But we had us some gin this morning," and he look at her real hard and he go over to the record player and he turn it on. It like he got to do something with his hands and he don't know what else to do.

Miss Lee don't say nothing. She just go to the kitchen
and she come back with two bottles of Pepsi Cola and
three glasses. And she fill a glass for WT and Blinky
and TJ.

But, then, all of a sudden, she start to cry.
"Why she crying?" TJ ask Blinky.
"She been sick," Blinky say, "She real sick."
WT look at Miss Lee and Mr Man and he start to

shivering again.

 Mr. Man say, real low and evil, between his teeth, "I been telling you about that roof. One of these days I'm going to have to put you away again."

Miss Lee stop crying and she walk over to WT and she take his face in her hands.

"Little man," she say. "Little man."

WT just stare at her, with her eyes real big. And then tears start rolling out his eyes.

Blinky say, "Come on, WT. You can walk, can't you?"

Miss Lee kiss WT, and she hold him in her arms for a minute. Then she move away and she look quick, just for a minute, at Mr Man. But WT watching. And TJ watching WT.

LITTLE MAN SHE SAY LITTLE MAN

And he more scared now than he ever been at Miss Beanpole's house. He more scared than he ever been before, and he don't know why.

Blinky's glasses just shining like diamonds.

Blinky look hard at WT and finally she say, just like she older than time, "You better start to walking, little man."

Then, she start moving, dancing to the music. She putting on a show for WT, really, she want to make him smile.

TJ watching WT.

Pretty soon, Blinky do something to the music to make Mr Man laugh. Then, Miss Lee laugh, and Mr Man put one arm around her shoulder. WT still just lying there, and watching. But then, TJ think *Shucks*, and he start into doing his African strut and WT just crack up.

Afterword

Aisha Karefa-Smart

U ncle Jimmy, Uncle Jimmy! When are you going to write a book about me?"

My mischievous little brother TJ, who was infamous for his antics and knew he was worthy of his own book, would ask my uncle this question whenever he saw him. It never occurred to me that amid all of our uncle's traveling, interviews, parties, and photo shoots (my uncle was one of the most photographed and therefore recognizable literary and civil rights icons), Uncle Jimmy would actually have the time to write a book about TJ. But my uncle was a promise keeper. And a promise was a promise. Even though he knew children's literature was a long stretch from his more heady works of literature, my uncle lovingly and meticulously penned his first and only children's book— and it was all about TJ. I never claimed the character "Blinky." But as my brother's keeper and big sister/constant companion I followed wherever he went, keeping a close eye as he went from adventure to adventure, up and down our busy neighborhood on Manhattan's Upper West Side. So Uncle Jimmy got that right, too.

When the box of books arrived from the original publisher, Dial Press, and we saw a little boy who looked just like TJ whimsically strut up and down the street as if it was his very own "Never-land," our eyes widened in awe. Uncle Jimmy really did write a book about TJ!!!! "Yay for TeeJayyy!!!!," we exclaimed. My brother asked and it was given. The type of love that was demonstrated by that one act let us all (the children in the family) know that we were very important to our uncle. We mattered. Our lives, our stories, what we did day in and day out as children was now chronicled in a children's book that other children, perhaps even children all over the world, would read. My little brother, who was beloved throughout our extremely multi-ethnic neighborhood, had his very own book in which my uncle lovingly captured his nephew's spirit.

But deep down, we knew he wrote it for all of us.

Contributors

JAMES BALDWIN (1924–1987), the world-famous novelist, playwright, essayist, critic, and public intellectual, was the grandson of a slave. He grew up in Harlem and was the oldest of nine children. He spent three years as a preacher while in his teens and briefly worked on the New Jersey railroad. In the 1940s he met his mentor, painter Beauford Delaney, and moved to Greenwich Village. In 1948 he left the United States and moved to Paris. His first novel—*Go Tell It on the Mountain*—was published in 1953, and for the next ten years he wrote many essays and several of his best-known works, including *Notes of a Native Son*, *Giovanni's Room*, and *The Fire Next Time*. During the 1960s Baldwin split his time between Istanbul and the United States, where he was active in the civil rights movement. In 1971 he moved to Saint Paul-de-Vence, a village in the south of France. There he wrote, among other works, *Little Man, Little Man*, which he dedicated to Beauford Delaney, and the novel *If Beale Street Could Talk*, which he dedicated to Yoran Cazac.

YORAN CAZAC (1938–2005) was a French artist who first gained attention for his abstract paintings in Paris in the 1960s. He moved to Rome, where he became the protégé of the painter Balthus, director of the French Academy. Cazac met Baldwin in Paris in 1959 through their mutual friend, painter Beauford Delaney. They rekindled their friendship in the 1970s, when Baldwin asked Cazac to provide the illustrations for *Little Man, Little Man*. Baldwin contributed an essay for the catalog of Cazac's 1977 exhibition at the Chateau de Maintenon. His final solo exhibition was held at the Kiron Gallery in Paris in 2003.

NICHOLAS BOGGS is a clinical assistant professor of English at New York University.

JENNIFER DEVERE BRODY is a professor of Theater and Performance Studies at Stanford University.

TEJAN KAREFA-SMART, James Baldwin's nephew, is a photographer and digital media artist who lives in Paris, France.

AISHA KAREFA-SMART, James Baldwin's niece, is an author who lives in Washington, D.C.